Who Said Meow?

Adapted from the Russian
by Maria Polushkin

Pictures by Giulio Maestro

Crown Publishers, Inc., New York

This book belongs to Puss
M.P.

Library of Congress Cataloging in Publication Data

Polushkin, Maria.
    Who said meow?

    Adaptation of V. G. Suteyev's Kto skazal "Miau"?
    SUMMARY: Puppy tries to find out which animal makes
the new sound he hears.
    [1. Animals—Fiction] I. Suteyev, Vladimir Grigor'-
evich. Kto skazal "Miau"? II. Maestro, Giulio, illus.
III. Title.
PZ7.P7695Wh3   [E]   74-19500
ISBN 0-517-518-465

Who Said Meow?

One morning, Puppy was sleeping
a sweet puppy sleep. Just above
his ears, he heard someone say,

"MEOW."

"It must have been a dream," he said, and he went back to sleep.

"MEOW."

Puppy couldn't sleep any more.
He *had* to see who was making
that noise.
He looked under the table.

He looked under the bed.

Then he climbed up on the
windowsill and looked outside.
Rooster was out for a stroll.
"Did you say MEOW?" asked Puppy.

"I don't ever say MEOW," said
Rooster. "I wouldn't say MEOW.
I say COCK-A-DOODLE-DOO."

"This is a bigger mystery than
I thought," said Puppy, and he went
outside to see what he could find.

"MEOW."

"It must be under the porch," said
Puppy, and he started to dig.

"Did you say MEOW?" said Puppy
to scared little Mouse.

"Oh no! I don't say MEOW.
I say SQUEAK SQUEAK," squeaked
Mouse, and he quickly ran away.

Then Puppy heard the sound
coming from the big doghouse.

"MEOW."

Puppy ran around the doghouse,
but no one was there.

Then he heard another noise.
"It's in there alright! Now I'm going
to catch it." And he ran inside.

Big Hairy Dog was in there, and he growled very loudly. "GRRRR." "Pardon me. Was it you, perhaps, er, ah, who said MEOW?" asked Puppy.

Big Hairy Dog opened his huge mouth, "GRRRRR   GRRRRRR   GRRRROWL!"

Puppy ran as quickly as he could.
He hid under a big thick bush.
Then right above his ears, he
heard it again.

"MEOW."

He peeked out from under the bush,
and there right in front of him
was fuzzy buzzy Bumble Bee.

Puppy lifted his paw to catch Bee.
He was sure that this was the one
who was making all that noise.

Bee got angry. "BUZZ BUZZZ BUZZ,"
it said, and it stung Puppy right on
the tip of his sweet puppy nose.

Puppy cried. He ran to the pond
and dove right in.

When he stuck his head out of
the water, Bee was gone, but that
same old noise was still there.

"MEOW."

"Was that you saying MEOW?" he asked Fish who was swimming by. Fish just flipped his tail and dove deeper into the water.

"CROAK CROAK CROAK," laughed
Frog from a nearby lily pad.
"You are dumber than I thought!"

"Well then, I don't suppose it was
you that said MEOW?" asked Puppy.

Frog just laughed and jumped
into the water.

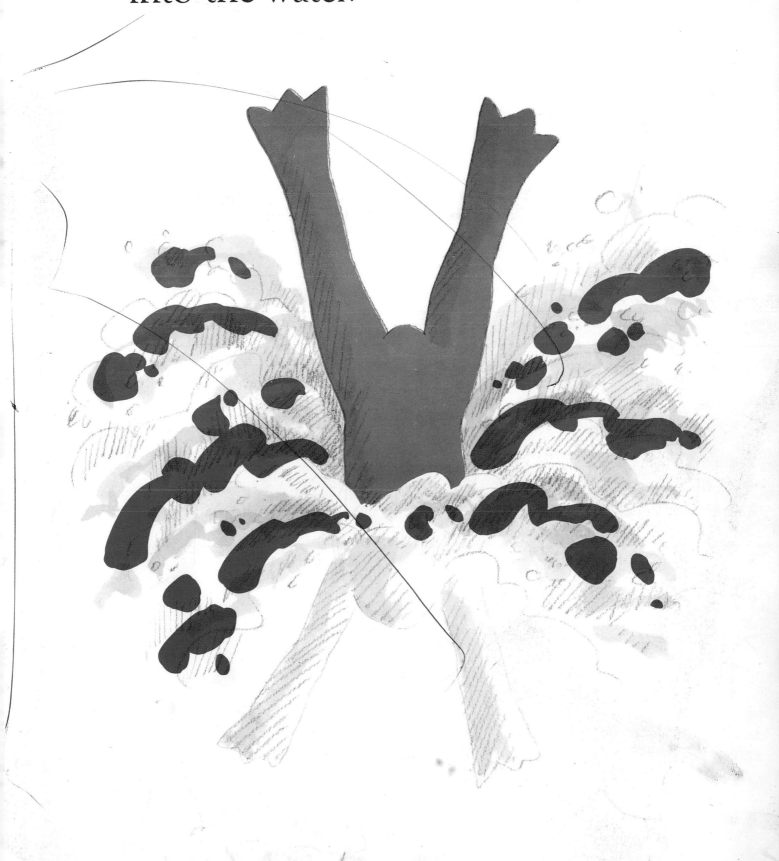

Poor Puppy. His sweet puppy fur
was wet, his sweet puppy nose was
swollen, and his puppy spirit was sad.

He dragged himself home and curled
up on the rug by the sofa and fell
into a troubled puppy sleep.

"MEOW."

Puppy woke up fast. There on the windowsill was the fluffiest old striped thing that you would ever want to see....

"MEOW," said Cat.

Puppy didn't say a word. He just laid himself right back down and curled himself right back up and went back to his sweet puppy sleep with a big smile on his sweet puppy face.